W9-AMV-566

HALLOWEEN HOWLS

HALLOWEEN HOWLS

Riddles that are a Scream
by Giulio Maestro

A Puffin Unicorn

DUTTON CHILDREN'S BOOKS
NEW YORK

Copyright © 1983 by Giulio Maestro
All rights reserved.
Unicorn is a registered trademark of
Dutton Children's Books.

Library of Congress number 83-1419
ISBN 0-14-036115-4

Published in the United States by
Dutton Children's Books,
a division of Penguin Books USA Inc.
375 Hudson Street, New York, New York 10014

Editor: Ann Durell   Designer: Giulio Maestro

Printed in Hong Kong by South China Printing Co.
First Unicorn Edition 1992
10 9 8 7 6 5 4

For Ann Durell

How do you keep flies out of a
haunted house?

Put screams in all the windows.

Why did the ghoul fail in school?
The teacher couldn't read his handwrithing.

What does a vampire put on when he gets out of a bat tub?

His bat robe.

When do ghosts have parties?
When they're dying to get together.

What animal can't be found in a haunted house?

A scaredy-cat.

Why did the ghost's car stop dead?
It ran out of gasps.

Why does a vampire nap in a closed coffin?

It helps him sleep tight.

What streets do ghosts haunt?
Dead ends.

How do vampires hit home runs?
With strong bat swings.

Why are skeletons empty-headed?
They have nothing between the ears.

How can you tell if a ghost is lying?

You can see right through him.

How do witches stay in touch?
By calling poison-to-poison on the telebone.

When does a ghost sleep in a graveyard?
When he's dead tired.

How does a skeleton study?
By boning up on the facts.

What is a chilling Halloween
dessert?

Bloodcurdling cream.

Why are vampires so serious?
They deal with grave matters.

When is a sorcerer's snake all wrapped up in itself?

When it's spellbound.

When does a skeleton laugh?
When something tickles his funny bone.

How did the witch feel when she fell off her broom?

Alarmed at the gravity of the situation.

What are creepy crawlies?
Snails dressed up for Halloween.

What is a vampire's favorite dish?
Transylvanian ghoulash.

Why don't you say "Trick or treat"
to an owl?

He doesn't give a hoot.

What animal does a ghost ride?
A nightmare.

What do you call a skeleton when he's not working?

Lazybones.

Why is a haunted house sad when it rains?

Its spirits are dampened.

How does a vampire make a sandwich?
With a loaf of dread.

What tops off a ghost's sundae?
Whipped scream.

What did the ghosts buy at the furniture store?

A deadroom set.

What exam do young witches have to pass?

A spell-ing test.

What are the ghosts of nightcrawlers?
Unearthly worms.

What happens when a ghost gets lost in a fog?

He's mist.

Why did the witch buy all the brooms in the store?

She liked to make sweeping decisions.

What does a musical ghost like to read?

Sheet music.

What does a jack-o'-lantern wear
over a sore eye?
A pumpkin patch.

What do little ghosts listen to before they go to sleep?

Deadtime stories.

What is a ghost in freezing rain?
A sheet of ice.

Why does a witch like to take rabbits for a ride?

It's a hare-raising experience.

What is a grizzly dressed as a ghost?

Bear-ly visible.

What does a sorceress wear?
A bewitching outfit.

What does a vampire say when his lunch is served?

"Fang you very much!"

When do ghosts ice-skate?
In the dead of winter.

Why are wizards so popular?
They have charming personalities.

Why does a vampire open his
valentine mail quickly?

To get to the heart of the matter.

Why did the ghoul's bicycle go so fast?

It had spooked wheels.

Where does a ghost refuel his car?
At the ghastly station.

What sailors like being chilled
to the bone?

A skeleton crew.

What do you send to a sick ghost?
Get-well witches.

What does a vampire drink on hot nights?

Something ghoul.

Why do ghosts like shooting galleries?

They're dead shots.

What kind of stories do boas like?

Gripping tales.

What kind of music do monsters play?

Violence concertos.

Why don't snakes need silverware?
They have forked tongues.

What happens when a spider takes
a fly for a ride?

They go for a spin.

What lake is scary?
Lake Erie.

Why was the mummy so tense?
He was all wound up.

Why did the hound try to bite the skeleton?

He had a bone to pick with him.

What is a ghost's Christmas treat?
Glum pudding.

Are werewolves' jokes funny?
They're a howl!